It's Too Much!

It's Too Much!

By Patty Wing Davis
Illustrated by Cindy Ho

Sometimes my grandpa gives
me a huge bowl of noodles.

I say, "Papa, it's too much!"

My grandma scoops
out a big bite,

and I feel better.

Sometimes my friend dares me
to jump from the tree house.

I say, "Hollis, it's too much!"

We throw our shoes off instead,

and I feel better.

Sometimes I see someone who
is sad, and I feel sad too.

I think, "Stop, it's too much!"

I send them kindness
and sparkles,

and I feel better.

Sometimes my dog wants
me to throw the ball forever.

I say, "Cleo, that's too much!"

I lie in the yard, and
she licks my face,

and I feel better.

Sometimes I feel like
I'm not in my body.

I think, "Body, it's too much!"

I go outside and
pretend to be a tree,

and I feel better.

Sometimes my mom
kisses me—a lot!

I say, "Momma, it's too much!"

We hug and snuggle,

and I feel better.

Sometimes I feel like other people's feelings are stuck on me.

I think, "Everyone, this is too much!"

I take a shower and wash away all
the feelings that aren't my own,

and I feel better.

Sometimes when there are too many people around I feel scared.

I think, "People, this is too much!"

I find a quiet place and take three
deep breaths,

and I feel better.

Sometimes I worry that there are scary things in my room.

I say, "Monsters, it's too much!"

I make myself big and bright
and yell, "Get out!"

and I feel better.

Sometimes my brother makes me
laugh until my side hurts.

I say, Cruz, it's too much!"

We lie in the grass and
watch the clouds,

and I feel better.

Sometimes everything feels
like it's too much.

I think, "World, this is too much!"

I put myself in a golden
bubble of safety,

and I feel better.

Sometimes the lady at the
store gives me an extra
large ice cream cone.

I say, "Thank you,"

I never say, "It's too much!"

Library of Congress Cataloging-in-Publication Data
Names: Davis, Patty Wing, author.
Title: It's Too Much! / words by Patty Wing Davis : Illustrated by Cindy Ho
Summary: Illustrations and easy-to-read text show an empathic child,
overwhelmed by circumstances, inventing clever ways to become calm.
Identifiers: LCCN 2022903781
ISBN 978-0-578-36644-9 (hardback) | ISBN 978-0-578-38975-2 (e-book)
Subjects: BISAC: JUVENILE FICTION / Social Themes / Emotions and Feelings | JUVENILE
FICTION /Family / General | JUVENILE FICTION /Social Themes/ Self Esteem
and Self Reliance.

ISBN 978-0-578-36644-9

Design by Cindy Ho. Text set in Andika New Basic
Illustrations rendered in Adobe Photoshop 2020

Printed in the U.S
by Wing & Aether Publishing
additional copies available at wingandaether.com

This book is dedicated to:

The extremly sensitive and empathic children

and

Dylan, Cedar and Indigo, my three empathically
sensitive offspring whose gifts have manifested in
wonderful ways.

About the Book

The goal of this book is to offer simple visualizations to help our extremely sensitive and empathic children find peace.

These are children that have the ability to sense, to be keenly aware of, to understand, and to share the thoughts, feelings and experiences of others.

While this gift gives birth to kind, caring and compassionate beings, it can also manifest as an emotional, energetic and sometimes physical burden.

As a psychic intuitive, I have many clients who are parents to these remarkable kids and have come to me searching for understanding and guidance on how to better support them.

It is important that we all build an awareness of what emotions and energies belong to us and what we may be absorbing from others. Through this discernment we learn to better understand and protect ourselves and find balance.

It is my sincere hope to offer insight and support to parents as well as to children through this book.

When we are able to control our empathy it becomes an intuitive gift that helps us navigate through our lives rather than something that victimizes or controls us.

Gratitude

I am deeply and sincerely thankful to my ever-supportive family, to my three children, Dylan, Cedar and Indigo. The love I have for you is deep, unconditional and purely magical.

Thank you, Cedar, for your patience and help with grammar, editing and ignorant computer questions.

Indigo, thank you for sharing your wisdom and telepathic under-standing of children.

Dylan, the creativity you weave into your daily life inspires me.

Gratitude to my personal cheerleader, husband Grant whose love, support and encouragement is strong and unwavering. You are my walking stick.

Thank you Kathy Wollenberg for your friendship, wisdom and assistance.

To my friend, chosen sister and illustrator Cindy Ho, you are ferociously talented and have shown an intuitive ability to read beyond my words. You have somehow portrayed my emotions and intentions into meaningful illustrations. I am in awe. This book would not have happened without your love and commitment. I am beyond grateful.

About the Author

Patty is a psychic intuitive and medium, spiritual teacher, aromatherapist, writer and podcaster living in Humboldt County in Northern California.

She has a thriving business, Wing and Aether, where she offers psychic readings and classes. Patty is also the co-host of Spirit Speakers Podcast, a program delving into a variety of metaphysical topics.

Patty considers herself an extreme empath. Once this gift started to manifest into anxiety, she began studying, meditating, and discovering tools that worked. She eventually achieved an awareness that remedied her anxiety, cultivated her current career to help others, and led her to author this book.

About the Illustrator

Cindy lives in Los Angeles and loves her dogs, Ella and Darla, her partner, Steve, and her partner in crime, Patty, not necessarily in that order.